Raj mein Gunde
Dharm mein Pande
Samaj mein Andhe

About the Author

Pitamber Pant grew up in a rural environment before moving to Delhi for his graduation. He did his PG in commerce and management accounting and started working as a management consultant in mid 80s. In 92, he co-promoted a management consulting firm and he has done consulting work with leading global and Indian organizations. He has travelled extensively in India and abroad.

Assisting family in agriculture sector during formative years, working in small stints with odd jobs during his higher education and then establishing himself as a successful management & HR consultant, he is a self-made man with great connect with rural India, industry and global fraternity. This is his first, perhaps the only book, and he gives a unique analysis for the current sad state of affairs of Bharat and a possible road map for regaining our pride of place in the world. The language is simple, contents absorbing and the message very meaningful.

Raj mein Gunde
Dharm mein Pande
Samaj mein Andhe

Pitamber Pant

ZORBA BOOKS

ZORBA BOOKS

Publishing Services in India by Zorba Books, 2019

Website: www.zorbabooks.com
Email: info@zorbabooks.com

Print Book ISBN 978-93-88497-48-0
E-Book ISBN 978-93-88497-49-7

Zorba Books Pvt. Ltd.(opc)
Gurgaon, INDIA

Tera tujhako arpan

Dedicated

Brahmleen Shri Anand Giri ji Maharaj

The Context

Growing up as an adult during the emergency era – experiencing the ruthless arrests, comic situations in *nasabandi* campaign, Mandal from VP Singh's kamandal creating a fragmented society, mindless deaths in the dance of democracy which continue unabated, and the compromised Prime Ministers in the last few years of 20th Century left me stunned and frustrated by the time I hit mid 30s. The situation hasn't improved – it has deteriorated further. Rampant loot, lies, no hold bar culture and absence of right leadership in the new century has created a severe feeling of frustration, helplessness and self-pity across India.

Majority of the ills flourished in 90s - corruption got institutionalized, Polity got fragmented and the Media became glamorous. It lost sense of what is worthy of propagation and what is not. By late 90s media was competing to become a Tabloid! R*espected* national publication like India Today publishing Wife Swapping as the cover story and Hindustan

Times carrying a front page story on how losing virginity in late teen was becoming the norm.

In 1990, a wandering monk who was for a long time in Rajgurunagar, Pune, landed close to my native place in Ranikhet and I had the good fortune of meeting him. He too was full of frustration looking at today's *Bharat* and his frequent utterance "Raj mein Gunde – Dharam mein Pande" was very thought provoking and I decided that one day I will write a book with this title. The Monk settled down in this place and whenever I visited my native place, I went to pay my reverence to him and heard the same dialogue again and again. Towards the end of 2004, the Monk added one more line to the title and told me that if I ever wrote a book, I should add *Samaj mein Andhe* to the title. And the Monk left his body in Dec 04 to move on with his journey.

What is the point in writing a book to bring out one's frustration - I pondered? Will it help in any way? Perhaps! Renewal of learning from the past would definitely be useful. As human beings, we suffer from loss of memory! We know the wonder of the wonders is the tendency of humankind to forget. Amply amplified by the 1st question of Yaksha to Yudhister, "What is the biggest wonder of the world?" and the answer, "Forgetful of human mind, it knows that the death is the most certain thing yet it remains forgetting it all the time".

May be this small initiative of mine will be of use for the future leadership and citizens to learn from the past! It may be read by some of the students of history in the future! It may inspire some of my countrymen to explore possibility of our returning to the lost glory - rebuild Bharat from India! And it will certainly take a big load off my back. As I had told the Monk that I will write the book.

I start writing this book with these thoughts on this 3rd navaratra day 30th Sept 11 – bowing to the Monk who left the body on 24th Dec 04. Who I could never address as Guru Ji because of not being worthy of a *Chela* but who blessed me and continues to bless me even today. I pray to the Goddess Saraswati to guide me in making this book achieve some of the objectives outlined above.

I thank my *bhanja* Sunil Joshi who helped in doing some media research and compilation work in between his CA exams. I am also indebted to Mr. Sunil Misra, who is more like an elder brother, to happily accept the editing work for the English edition.

May the Almighty bless us all with the power of bringing Bharat back to its lost glory!

Pitamber Pant Pantgaon, Almora.

P.S. Post Sept 11, I had the call of my *karmic* debts in the shape of illness, house getting constructed, acute health problems at home and so on. But the road to election of 2014 again pushed my lazy mind & body to go back to the writing. Will the election of 2014 bring a compromised formula *gathbandhan* - or should we call it *sathbandhan* – because everyone is there to get a piece of the booty and not to serve the nation and society! The worst would be if Prime Minister positon changes hands amongst the alliance partners! In a country of 1.30 billion people, it's a pity that we are suffering because of misguided leadership!

So here I go again and hope that this time I accomplish this goal and live up to the promise I made to the great Monk, Brahmleen Shri Anand Giri ji Maharaj –and if this happens it will be only because of his blessings and the grace of *Ma Saraswati.*

As I thought of completing the book, the election took place and we had a Govt with a clear majority and a Prime Minister who the people thought will bring the changes in the way of Governance, drive the corruption out of the system and lead the country to its past glory. I too thought that there was a good possibility of this happening and hence the writing of the book again took a back seat. Looking at the balance sheet of the current Govt, the urge to complete the book has again revived and at last I handover the manuscript to Mr. Misra for editing on the auspicious day of Posh Purnima, the 21st Jan 19.

Contents

The Trigger

My father was someone who deserted British Army to join INA on the call of Neta ji Subhash Chandra Bose. Whenever my father went through the sweet silent thoughts of freedom movement, he felt very aggrieved as he thought that post freedom, the country had become more colonial. I as a teenager had difficulty in understanding this. The emergency followed and I was in my final year of graduation. The young lot felt cheated and I too was part of this angry lot. The students' movement under Late Jai Prakash Narayan brought the desired fruits and Mrs. Gandhi and her Congress had to bite the dust in 77 elections. However, the greed for power brought the Government down in 18 months. Mr. Charan Singh who wanted Mrs. Gandhi to be punished and put behind bars in Haryana, overnight accepted her proposal to withdraw support to Morarji Desai's Government and instead form his own Government with the support of Congress. He believed in her and did what she wanted. And at nick of the time, when it came to testing the strength in the Parliament, she refused the support. I as a young person felt very angry with both of them. With Late Ch Charan

Singh because he was totally swayed away by the greed of power, and Mrs. Gandhi because she spoke a lie to the entire country. She gave a written letter to the President and withdrew it in 48 hours on the eve of the floor test in the Parliament. A leader of her stature speaking such a lie – what is the message to the masses!

Another incident in 1990 made me really upset at our current system. I happened to be in my native place around Panchayat elections time. People in the village had to field a very simple and poor man as a candidate for Gram Pradhan to challenge a tough guy. I was pushed into becoming the poor man's Polling Officer. As I was on duty at the polling station, I noticed three beautiful girls coming to vote for the second time. This time they wore different dresses and were giving different names of themselves and their fathers/husbands. If they had not been pretty and had not come together again, I would not have noticed.

Voting process got stopped and suddenly I heard noises outside the polling booth. When I came out, I saw my colleague i.e. second polling officer – a retd army person in his 60s, was surrounded by a group of men and they were all set to beat him. I intervened and succeeded in saving my fellow officer. The voting got restarted after sometime. The next morning I came to know that there was a death in another polling booth at a distance of about 20 Kms. The death of dozens in elections in W Bengal all the time, reconfirm the extent of *goondaism* in our polity. All in the name of democracy and elections!

The final trigger has been the BJP Government of Mr. Vajpayee at the Center. First the episode of Kargill! Our then Prime Minister was dreaming for the Noble Prize and so he allowed Pakis to settle down at the position of advantage despite warnings from the Media and the Army. Finally our brave young men in the Army made it to the top of the hills, after sacrificing so many lives. Instead of letting the Army teach the invaders a lesson, we provided them safe passage. I think it was the only war with Pakistan where we first allowed them to take the position of advantage and then did nothing to teach them a lesson.

And finally then the declaration of *aar-paar ki larai* and sending troops to borders – troops are stationed in war mode at borders for nine months and then withdrawn. The country's prestige had suffered like never before.

However, Dr Manmohan Singh became Prime Minister and the book again took a back seat as one really hoped that there will be some cleansing under his leadership. While his first stint was average except for the stand he took on Nuclear agreement, the second stint has been soaked in corruption stories – CWG, 3G, Coalgate, Railgate, etc. We know it was partly by design of the opposition but his ministers too were not under his control and a free for all atmosphere prevailed.

The 2014 election brought back the hope that things may change. However, nothing has changed. The scenario has only worsened. I now can't stop but write my feelings about our downfall and the reasons thereof. Is this the state of affairs our forefathers wanted? What have we done to the sacrifices of those thousands who laid their lives from 1857 to 1947 – a struggle of 100 years? No, sorry – not 100 years but right from the time the country was occupied by Mughals. Shivaji, Guru Gobind Singh, Maharana Pratap, Tantyaji, Mangal Pande, Jhansi Ki Rani, Chander Shekhar Azad, Raj Guru, Bhagat Singh and the multitude of people from across the country.

The book has two parts – 1st describing the post independence leadership and how it has almost destroyed an ancient culture in 70 years and the second half on the path ahead to restore the glory of the motherland.

Analysis of
post-independence
leadership

◆◆◆

M ost of us have read Lord Macaulay's
address to the British Parliament in 1835.
To refresh our memory, let us go through the
speech once again:

"I have travelled across the length and
breadth of India and I have not seen one person
who is a beggar, who is a thief – such wealth
I have seen in this country, such high moral
values, people of such caliber that I don't think
we would ever conquer this country unless we
break the very backbone of this nation, which
is her spiritual and cultural heritage, and,
therefore, I propose that we replace her old and
ancient education system, her culture, for if the
Indians think that all that is foreign and English
is good and greater than their own, they will
lose their self-esteem, their native culture and
they will become what we want them, a truly
dominated nation.."

What he describes is a true Ram Raj and
what the British couldn't accomplish, we have
managed to do i.e. break the backbone in70
years of independence! Who is responsible for

this? Is it society or the leadership? You talk to people at the helm of affairs in any organ of our Govt. and the reply is that what can we do - we have to manage with the people the society produces.

So we are back to the puzzle of egg first or the chicken first! Is society influencing the leadership or is it the reverse? Definitely the reverse! The Lord in Gita (3/21) clearly confirms this:

"Yaddhath Aachrati Shrestha, tattad evetaro janah. sa yat parmaana kurute, lokas tad anuvartate"

The Lord says that the behavior of people, who are Shreshta of the time, becomes the standard for the rest. Therefore the leadership is responsible for destroying the culture and heritage of this country. In Indian context, the Shreshta of the time is the PRIME MINISTER and his team! Analyzing the leadership of the last 70 years, and identify each Prime Minister's role in creating today's India from Bharat of 1832 – the year when Lord Macaulay visited India, therefore is important. It is not an individual but the Prime Minister, the Shreshta, of the time which is being analyzed. Not for criticizing but to illustrate the truth in the Lord's wisdom.

Nehru – a nationalist in western mould

Let us first look at a few positives of Mr. Nehru. He had total belief in democracy and its institutions including Parliament. Hs respected them, nourished them and if we are still a thriving democracy; a lot of credit goes to him as our first and long time prime minister. The second important contribution from him was establishing India in the leadership gallery of the world including starting the Non Aligned Movement.

Nehru was a nationalist but his upbringing was in a foreign land. Cultural shift started happening immediately after independence. Nehru time and again reminded people that we are an old culture and we need to change to keep pace with the world. Someone who had his upbringing in the UK and hardly understood the *Sanatan* philosophy, started changing the Bharat to India by telling the society to shun the old culture and adopt the new one. His famous address to the nation was, "Old as we are, with memories stretching back to the early dawns of human history and endeavour, we have to grow young, in tune with our present time.."

He would not have been the Prime Minister if Gandhi ji didn't have a soft corner for him. Gandhi ji was Dronacharya and Nehru his Arjun! Gandhi ji took a promise from all the

11

senior members of Congress before dying that they will never oppose Nehru after his death. It is well documented that people like Patel and Kriplani wanted to oppose Nehru number of times but kept mum because of the promise they had made to Bapu! So we got our first Prime Minister who didn't understand the Sanatana philosophy, thought India was backward and the derailment of the country started.

Let us look at a few major decisions which Mr. Nehru took:

Hindu Personal Law: This is the first piece of legislation which he fought for over a period of time as there was huge opposition to it from his own party. He started the move right in 1948 and continuously fought for it till it got passed in 1955. In June 1948, constituent assembly's own president Rajendra Prasad warned the prime minister that to introduce 'basic changes' in personal laws was to impose the 'progressive ideas' of a 'microscopic minority' on the Hindu community as a whole. Nehru answered that the cabinet had cleared the bill and that "personally I am entirely in favour of the general principles embodied in it. To scrap the legislation now would be to give rise to the suspicion that the congress was a reactionary and a very conservative body; nor would it go down well in the mind of foreigners outside India'. Prasad shot back that the opinion of the vast Hindu public were more important than the views of foreigners. The bill thus was inspired by the western view of life which attaches more value to the romance of marital relation and married life rather than to parenthood in which marriage attains its fruition. The Hindu system conceives of parenthood as something that is permanent, unchangeable, and inviolable.

Institution of Marriage was sacred in this land, arranged by applying time tested scientific parameters and disputes if any were settled through the relations. Why was this so urgent for him? Against the very spirit of Hindu Civilization, the bill was inspired by the western view of life where marriage is romance rather than an important institution for building a cultured society and a stepping stone to spiritual growth. **So the first damage was done** - the popular psychology towards the sanctity of marriage and *garhasth ashram* was changed.

Changing the Education System: The other blunder was playing around with the education system. The education pattern got changed – a task which was not even touched by earlier foreign rulers – whether Mugals or British. Sanskrit was

13

given a back seat. The number tables were intact in the fraction form till independence and we changed them to simpler tables in mid 50s. I think the fraction tables had enormous contribution to develop analytical faculties of individuals. During the British Raj, if a Commissioner went on leave, the charge was given to the Principal of the Inter College of the district. The teaching community therefore was highly respected and it lost its respect progressively in the free India.

Exploitation of the nature: Nehru believed like most of the western economists did - that development was synonymous with the exploitation of nature. For him the western world stood for the civilization. So the landscape started getting changed –dams blocked rivers, mining was taken up in a big way and *swadeshi & cottage industries dream* of Gandhi ji was forgotten. We now have rivers which do not flow – some of which still flow give a feeling of garbage slurry. Fertility of land has evaporated with chemicals and genetic seeds, and whatever land is left is getting shifted to industrial & commercial use.

Nehru thus sowed the seeds of cultural change – propagating western culture & development model and changing the education system – Sanskrit taking a back seat and English in the front.

14

Shastri – the real hero

Coming to my own memories of beyond 1965, I clearly remember how Shri Lal Bahadur Shastri energized each person in this country at a time of despair – *akaal* on one hand and *war* by Pakistan on the other. His slogan of "Jai Jawan – Jai Kisan" became very popular. This was truly in sync with the nature of this great land or should we say in line with Sanatan philosophy. Jawan to protect the country and Kisan to protect all living organisms. It is unfortunate but true that all good things do not last for long and we lost Shastri ji, a true Sanatani soul – special gift of the god.

He made us proud by winning the war in 1965 with poor preparation and equipment. When he was asked as to how to respond to the American Tanks deployed by Pak Army since we didn't have comparable weapons, his response was *Eat ka jabab Pathar se* and it saw .303 rifles giving befitting reply to the tanks.

His response to shortage of food grains was as inspiring. He advised all the citizens to keep a day's fast on Tuesday. And it became a ritual during his time and even the road side Dhabas were closed on Tuesday. He also asked everyone to use whatever piece of land they have for

15

growing food grains! The food problem was tackled to some extent with these innovative and enlightened thoughts and actions.

High on moral values – resigning as a Railway Minister when a rail accident took place, practicing *aprigraha* – only a few kgs of food grain in the house when he died and truthful to the core are the values he displayed. He thus is the real Hero of post independent India and there are no parallels till now.

What the brief tenure of Shastri ji proved was that you require a person of virtues – *yamas and niyamas* to run the country and the masses will respond. Again Lord's message - "Yadadh Aachrate Shrestha….." coming to life.

Indira – start of corruption & criminalization in politics!

Indira Gandhi was a true nationalist and a forceful leader. She was also a visionary e.g. she was not chasing the growth number – she knew development beyond a certain stage leads to destruction! She also kept the society intact – did not divide the society on caste and creeds, respected tribal rights and by and large national interest was her big priority. Taking the world head on during

1971 war and winning it is a great example of her leadership. A decision on nationalization of banks is another example of her boldness. Implementing the Green Revolution is another feather in the cap. Overall, she took decisions keeping long term interest of the nation in mind.

But the mixture of *Shakti* (energy) inherent in a female, and absolute power – no control; always proves lethal. It is well documented in the scriptures and also flows from *shruti* that a female which is the fountainhead of energy - *shakti* should never be given total independence! The 4 stubborn categories include *bal, triya, raj* and *yog hats*! With Leadership in her hands, she demolished individuals and institutions which came in her way. Thus with Indira's coming to the power ended the saga of value-based politics.

She started the license raj and success of a business man was not dependent on the business skills & acumen but whether you can get a license or not. Loans from financial institutions & banks came to people with the licence rather than the right business proposition. Results - more & more new businesses going sick or running inefficiently and citizens paying the price for this. You needed Government permission for everything – right from installing a generator,

17

getting something imported, overseas visits, getting a telephone installed or cooking gas connection. This led to a culture of middleman for the general public and a liaison man for the corporate world. And bribes became a done thing. No file would move unless you gave it fuel i.e. money and the saga of corruption started.

In fact one can safely say that both *corruption & criminalization* started with Mrs. Gandhi and then spread across all the sections of Government including Army & Judiciary. I happened to meet a retired army officer, Lt Col Khare, sometime in 1995. This gentleman was one of the seven POWs who were successful in running from China's custody after 1962 war. When the first shipment of tanks from Russia came to India in 1971, he was heading the inspection wing in the Eastern Command and Late Gen Vaidya was the DG Inspection (Brig) at that point of time. When this officer started inspecting the tanks, to his surprise, he found that most of them were used and second hand. He told the Russian officials that this was not what they were supposed to deliver! The Russian officials told him to check with the Prime Minister and not to ask them any questions. The officer was furious and submitted a report confirming that the supplies were not of acceptable standards.

He got a call the next day from Brig Vaidya summoning him to Delhi. He came to Delhi from Calcutta and was told by Brig Vaidya that the PM wants to meet him and that he should be ready for all eventualities. He was taken to PMO the next morning and after introduction by Brig Vaidya, he was left alone with the PM. Mrs. Gandhi complimented him for his great record and made brief talks about the family. She then took out a copy of the report and asked the officer to change it and in reward he could have a career of his choice either as head of a PSU or as a military attaché in Europe or US.

He told Mrs. Gandhi that there are 3 copies dispatched by him to different locations and changing one copy won't help. She took out the balance 2 copies from her drawer and put them in front of him. The officer had thought through the consequences before meeting her and told her that he will not be able to do this and would prefer to resign. He took out the already written resignation letter. Mrs. Gandhi asked him to re think and when the reply was again in negative, she asked him to make a promise to her. He agreed and the promise taken was that he would not talk to anyone about this meeting till the time she was alive. She shook his hand as reconfirmation of the promise and asked him to take the resignation and submit it through proper channel.

The corruption in army had begun. I was sitting at home of a close relation to congratulate his son who was coming from Dehradun after passing out from IMA. He was a rank holder in NDA as well as in IMA. The rank holders (the first 20 cadets) till early 80s were given a corps of their choice. This young cadet came home, was hugged by his father and after the preliminaries, was asked about the corps he had opted for. He told his father that it was ASC. The father was taken aback and enquired as to why he did not opt for a fighting arm!

The father was from the Ordinance and expected his son to join the same corp or at least a fighting arm. The reply he got was that ASC is the most preferred posting as on date and people even pay money for this. He was lucky to have a choice and what is wrong if he has opted for the most preferred corp. I left the place soon and prayed to the almighty for saving this great country. IMA changed the rules after observing this for a few years and as on date only topper from each of the 5 houses is given the choice against 20. Full credit to the Army for taking corrective action – I am so happy that they have their own judicial system and it works. It is unfortunate that higher courts are now entertaining cases and interfering in the defence establishments when they have no clue of the ground situations!

Let us take Mrs. Gandhi's rule little further. During the Bangladesh war, she clearly showed a lot of courage and determination and we did win the war. She got accolades from every quarter and won the next election with a huge majority. This made her totally autocratic. Anyone within the party, government, media or anywhere criticizing her, had to be taught a lesson. The following actions prove her autocratic behavior:

The chief minister of congress ruled states were chosen by the local legislators alone. However after the congress split in 1969, Mrs. Gandhi was able to place her own candidates in key positions and terminate them at her will. In 1971, after her spectacular victory in the election, she sacked in quick succession, the chief minister of Rajasthan and Andhra Pradesh, replacing them with her own favorites. In March 1973 the government appointed a new Chief Justice of the Supreme Court, Justice A.N.Ray and three colleagues ahead of him in seniority were ignored – a tradition betrayed.

The impatience with democratic institutional frame work resulted in the imposition of emergency. Now with opposition MPs locked away, a series of constitutional amendments were passed to prolong Mrs. Gandhi rule .The 38th amendments passed on 22nd July 1975, barred judicial review of the emergency . The 39th amendments introduced two weeks later stated that the election of the Prime Minister could not be challenged by Supreme Court. This came just in time to help Mrs. Gandhi in her election review petition and the court held that there was no case to try since the new amendments kept her out of the purview of law as a Prime Minister .

She continued to play around with Congress ruled states and also started interfering in the states not ruled by Congress. Dismissal of Farooq Abdullah's government in Jammu and Kashmir and a month later a change of regime was effected in Andhra Pradesh in 1984. The dismissal of the J&K and Andhra chief minister were very unfortunate violation of democratic practice. One cannot rule out personal vindictiveness as NTR and Farooq had first initiated the moves for opposition unity.

When Indira Gandhi came to power in January 1966, India was a coherent nation and the political class recognizing their key role as doing good for the nation and the society at large. But under her leadership the government at the center became corrupt, criminal conspiracies were rampant and the country was in poor state of affairs. Moral of the story – all that starts at the top, has to trickle down and the corruption & criminalization started soaking the fabric of the institutions including Army during her time. Again salutation to the Lord, "Yadadh Aachrate Shrestha .....".

Janata Party – beginning of Dhritrastra politics

Jai Prakash Narain was able to bring all the opposition leaders under one roof and galvanize the country to throw the Indira congress out of power. There was huge surge in the masses for throwing Mrs. Gandhi out and the country was behind the Jai Prakash movement. However, some leaders like George Fernades started violent protests – the Baroda Dynamite episode resulted in complete destruction of the Arrah telephone exchange and the severe damage to the railway system in 1975. These kinds of violent events gave Mrs. Gandhi a good excuse to declare emergency. All the leaders – right from district level to those at Delhi, were arrested or had fear of getting arrested.

Finally emergency got lifted and elections took place in March 1977. Janata Party won and Morarji Desai became the Prime Minister with two Dy Prime Ministers – Jagjivan Ram and Charan Singh. Jai Prakash's health was already bad and he didn't have time and energy to monitor the newly formed Govt and party. Janata Party came into being because of merger of a large number of small and medium sized political parties including the breakaway from Indira Congress like Samata Party of Jagjivan Ram and they were not cohesive. Infightings started – Jagjivan Ram and Charan Singh were made Dy Prime Ministers.

Ch. Charan Singh who was after Indira – wanted her to be arrested and put behind bars but got fooled by Mrs. Gandhi. He was promised the Prime Minister position with the support of Congress if he came out of Janta Party with his supporters. He agreed and withdrew from Janata Party – Morarji Govt came into minority and resigned. Mrs. Gandhi gave in writing to the President that her party supports Chaudhry

Saheb and when it came to prove its strength on the floor of the parliament, she withdrew support. Charan Singh Govt also fell. A national leader of her status speaking a blatant lie and taking pride in this! Expecting a truthful society when you have this kind of leadership is day dreaming.

So the Janta Party episode came to an end. Leaders not talking about their country but their pound of flesh. Dhritrastra politics - what is right for me and my family matters. The interest of the country took a back seat. People had big hopes, students like me lost educationally and got admonished at home for going berserk in support of the JP movement. It was a total let down by the leaders. Elections took place after 18 months and Indira Congress was back in power.

Rajiv – breath of fresh air

The assassination of Mrs. Gandhi in 1984 brought Rajiv Gandhi as the Prime Minister. The general election took place the next year and he won with a decisive majority. Rajiv was a man in a hurry – 40 years old who came into politics reluctantly and had good appreciation of the ills of the systems. The prime minister moved swiftly to make peace in the Punjab. The leaders of the Akali Dal were let out of jail and Sant Harcharan

Singh Longowal and Rajiv Gandhi signed a peace accord in July 1985. He also clinched an agreement with the All-Assam students union. President rule was ended and election called. In June 1986 the government of India signed a peace agreement with Laldenga, the leader of the Mizo National Front. In all these states, power did not come to Congress but it strengthened the democracy – so Rajiv was aggressively undoing the misdoings of his mother. And of course he visited China, a visit after a gap of more than 30 years by an Indian Prime Minister. The one major problem caused by him or by his party colleagues in collusion with Farooq Abdullah, was rigging of elections in J&K in 87 which caused an irreparable damage to the J&K situation.

One of the new prime minister's more daring departures was on the economic front. The Government budget, introduced in March 1985, sought to remove some of the control and checks in what was one of the tightly regulated economies in the world. The trade regime was liberalized and the licensing regime was simplified and deregulated. The Indian economy, said the prime minister in February 1985, had got "caught in a vicious circle of creating more and more controls. Controls led to all the corruption, to all the delays, and that is what we want to cut out".

It is indeed very rare that someone would change the policies adopted by his mother by 180 degree. He wanted to take India to the gallery of developed countries and recognized that communication was the key to this. So he brought Mr. Sam Pitroda as an advisor who revolutionized the telecom sector. Today the IT & Telecom is one of the largest employment providers. India is a key player in IT domain which is the driving force for innovation in other domains as well. There is one IT professional employed overseas across from each locality of India. Mr. Pitroda is hailed by people who have worked with him as an outstanding boss, human being and continues to serve the nation.

Rajiv opened Aviation, Manufacturing, Banking, etc to the private sector. To get a flight at a day's notice was impossible – corporate had liaison managers for this purpose. You only had an Ambassador or a Fiat as car brands. After booking a car, you would have to wait for upwards of 6 months and at the end you may not get the colour you wanted. Today you have regular flights and you can buy a car right when you need with finance available, get a phone or internet connection on demand, book your train ticket on net and the list goes on. Rajiv is the person who put this foundation in place.

He was worried about the caliber we were attracting to our civil and Defence services. He revised salaries, working conditions and was successful to a certain extent in attracting good talent into these services. He also discovered that only 25 paise out of a rupee is used for development and the rest is siphoned out! He knew it was a chain right from top to the banking or treasury guy who disburses the funds. It is not that it was unknown to those in the power since they were part of the beneficiaries but it is Rajiv who talked about it openly. His appointment of VP Singh as Finance Minister proved to be his undoing. Mr. V P Singh maligned him and back stabbed him on the Bofors gun deal. Some others in the party joined his band wagon and with the support of opposition who Rajiv had snubbed, pulled his Govt down to form the next Govt.

VP – Power hungry

V P Singh came to power by ditching Rajiv. He claimed that Rajiv's relations in Italy, late Quattrochi made huge money in the Bofors deal and that he would bring every one responsible to justice within 6 months. Commissions have been made in defence deals everywhere including India. These are long gestation period projects, need close follow up and the ability to influence the decision making technically and financially. Therefore there are people who do this liaison work for defence deals as in Bofors. Quattrochi's accounts were traced but money flowing out of his accounts did not find a link to Rajiv's family. It continues to be a political topic till today though Quattrochi expired in 2013.

Since V P Singh was not able to bring anything out in the open, a promise on which he became the Prime Minister, he started finding other vulnerable topics which would ensure that he remained in power even in the future. So he took out the Mandal Commission report which was commissioned by Mrs. Gandhi long back but put in the cold storage because of its ramifications. Ramifications which would distort the society and there would be demand for reservations all around. V P Singh now wanted to become a *Masiha* of the backwards, dalits, minorities and all other classifications of Mandal report.

The first salvo was reservations in education institutions and students across northern India organized rallies and demonstrations against it. The rallies turned violent and there were number of self immolations in protest. Instead of telling the youngsters to cool down and come for discussions, V P Singh and his Govt sought to defend themselves, sometimes to deadly effect. Incidents of police firing were reported from six states of the union claiming more than fifty lives. He did come on the Television only to reinforce that he will not budge! Youths are burning themselves and this guy doesn't get moved. No compassion!

So VP Singh started with reservations left, right and center! Brought mediocrity everywhere and created parties around the Mandal classifications. The reservations then took different colour – now reservations for handicapped, disabled, ladies and so on. The great Bharat today is getting ruled not by merit and competence but reservations! China is considered far ahead in diplomacy because it has very well groomed and intelligent diplomats and India is thinking of reserving some diplomatic positions for handicapped! When you have many people with two eyes, why will you appoint a blind man! This is totally against the law of the nature and the country is paying a price for this. Female reservation in defence is another funny problem. The judiciary has been championing this but doesn't know the ground realities on the frontiers. If males are better equipped to live with the wear & tear of frontiers, why have females!

One reads in the newspapers that some of the students who have got admissions in institutes of higher learning based on reservations are committing suicides. The human life is precious and children are the future of the nation. It is true that any one will find it difficult to find a place among top rankers if s/he is not of the same caliber. You get isolated, go into depression and commit suicide. It is very unfortunate for the one who is dying, and more so for the family and the society at large.

So the reservation Pandora box was opened by V P Singh which divided the society so much that integrating it will be a very difficult task for years to come. The disease continues to spread its wings and we have now Jats, Patels, Marathas, etc rallying for reservation and more will follow. When elections were held, none of this benefited him and we had a compromised leadership ruling the country for some time. V P Singh thereafter became sick and towards end of his life, was in great pain and agony! He had said once in his interview that every time he goes for a dialysis, he prays for death but his wish is not granted.

Lobho nashasya karanam! The hunger and greed destroyed himself, the Congress and the country. Animosity was created between different casts – the Bahujan Samaj Party came with a slogan of *"tilak, taraju aur talwar – inko maro jute char"*. Polity became very fragmented and we saw its ill effects in leadership and corruption in the last 3 decades. So VP gave us a fragmented society, compromised leadership and brought mediocrity in all walks of life. And Bharat continues to suffer because of these ills.

Narsimha Rao – institutionalization of corruption

The compromised Govts. Of VP Singh and Chandrasekhar didn't last long and elections were called in 1992. Rajiv got assassinated in one of the election meetings in Tamilnadu. Congress came out as a largest party and decided to elect Narsimha Rao as the Prime Minister with support of some other parties and independents. Narsimha Rao was all set to go for a heart operation and was not in great health. Narsimha instead of going to US for treatment came to 7 Race Course Road.

People give him credit for managing the economic growth with Dr Manmohan Singh as his Finance Minister. The global recession had just hit the trough and was in the upward movement, the blue print for opening the economy was already in place and approved by Congress Party during Rajiv's time, and Dr Singh was a brilliant economist. So things fell in place. He did a good job of handling the terror problem in Punjab. No doubt, he was a seasoned politician and an able administrator.

However, he used money to corrupt one and all. To get the majority, he had to buy some MPs including Shibu Soren of the JMM and his colleagues. The economy had to open up. Congress had this in the agenda because of Rajiv's vision. He started collecting money for favoring a few - brief cases getting delivered to 7 Race Course became a done thing. The economy was moving fast and so was corruption. Sukh Ram's, the then telecom minister house was raided and found full of currency notes. Prime Minister's sons, relatives and colleagues were all under scanner and later on tried in the court.

Mr. Narsimha Rao created an inferiority complex syndrome in the Govt circles for being honest! Right from peon to the Cabinet Secretary if you didn't make money, you were not the enlightened one. One Sunday morning, I was looking forward to my morning cup of tea after completing the daily drill. I got a call and the person said that he was calling from Telephone Exchange and that his lady boss would like to speak with me. I requested him to connect and the lady came on the line. She told me that I was making number of overseas calls and she had a proposal - whenever I need to make a call, I will get connected through the exchange and will have to pay only 50% of the cost to the exchange team. I was in no mood to argue or lose my temper to a lady on a Sunday morning and I told her that my residence phone belongs to my office and I have nothing to do with the payment as it is handled by the accounts guy. She wanted the name and telephone number of the gentleman concerned. I disconnected and realized that our Prime Minister has really institutionalized the corruption right up to the grass root.

He put the MPs at large in good mood and improved their earnings including starting with the MP Development Fund which was Rs 2 crores when started and is today at Rs 5 crores per annum. This is mainly responsible for getting criminals and businessmen to politics and institutionalizing the corruption.

As he was coming under clouds of corruption, one after another, he did a stupid thing of initiating CBI investigation against large number of leaders. The basis was a diary recovered which listed names of top politicians from congress as well as the opposition with amounts paid to them. He thought that he will finish his opposition within and outside congress with this move. It boomeranged badly and also isolated top congress leaders who then formed their own parties – N D Tiwari in UP, Arjun Singh & Kamal Nath in MP and Raja & Chidambaram in Tamilnadu. However, when election took place in 97, Congress was nowhere close to forming the Govt and Narsimha Rao back on earth.

So the corruption, wide and rampant today got institutionalized during the rule of Narsimha Rao and is his gift to the nation. "Yadadh Aachrate Shrestha....."

Atal Bihari – casualty of casualness!

Atal Bihari was a poet and a great orator. People of my generation were fond of his speeches. He was a well meaning gentleman with good intentions but not able to function under pressure. He was at his best in reciting poems. His first Govt could not get support when he had to prove the majority on the floor. Elections were held again and this time, BJP formed a coalition Govt of 13 parties which had Mamta and Jayalalitha as allies. After he won the vote in the parliament, late Rajesh Pilot participating in the discussions wished him well but said that he was at loss to understand how a person who didn't even manage a family, will manage such a large country and coalition. Pilot was on dot as Atal ji was made to dance by allies including three ladies – Mamata, Uma Bharti and Jayalalitha as well as Parvez Musharaf, the CEO of Pakistan.

A few good things for which he will be remembered are Pradhan Mantri Gram Sadak Yojana, managing the UTI fiasco, cancelling all the petrol pumps which were allotted to preferred parties and not coming under pressure for selling Indian Oil to private parties. He also brought Late Abdul Kalam as President of India and had a competent council of ministers.

His first test was tackling the hijack of Indian Airlines plane. Letting the flight go out of Indian Territory and then exchanging the dreaded terrorists in exchange has been the most unfortunate decision. Masood remains the biggest headache for our security forces since then. He started assembling group of Jehadis and training them with the help of ISI. All major infiltrations and attacks are attributed to his efforts and outfits.

On the Pakistan front, he was trying to figure out if he could solve the dispute with the Pakistan and may be win Noble Prize! The Govt went for a nuclear test right in the second month of its existence and its top ministers started saying that Pakistan should understand our strengths! The Pakis managed their test within a few days and did one more explosion than India. At this stage Vajpayee adopted a reconciliatory approach and went to Lahore with the inaugural bus in Feb 99. As he was busy in the discussion, 64 people were shot dead in Jammu. The PM should have returned but he stayed for another day to sign the accord with Pakistani PM – he was totally sold on the promises of Nawaz Sharif. He was a parliamentarian for ages and yet didn't understand how Pakistan is ruled!

Let us look at another major lapse by his Govt. The Indian army was first alerted on the infiltration in Kargil by a group of Indian shepherds. They had spotted men in pathan dress digging bunkers. They conveyed the information to the nearest regiment. Soon the army found that the Pakistanis had occupied positions across a wide swath of Kargil sector. Army reported the matter and wanted permission for an offensive. Army was advised to relax as Nawaz Sharif had promised to resolve the issue. In 1999, a documentary was commissioned for Ladakh sector by DD and when the documentary team went to the location, they were told about Pakistani build up by locals and it was recorded. When the tape was given to DD and they reviewed it, they reported the contents to the Govt. It was asked to put the tape on hold and again no action was taken.

May be Atal and Nawas had all good intentions. However, ignoring the ground reality and warnings after warnings, is utter casualness! The Pak army continued with their build up and started the attack once they had taken position on the top and had enough manpower and supplies with them. Nawaz was thrown out of power by military under Gen Mushrraf – the author of the Kargil. Kargil was totally mishandled and when it was time to punish the enemy, it was given safe passage. A golden opportunity to punish the enemy hard so they don't dare to look at us with an evil eye again was missed. The experience of 65 and 71 could have been repeated as the army was fully ready and so was the country. *Kavis* normally have a *komal* heart but that is bad for a ruler.

After General Mushrraf took over the regime as a CEO and was in Agra for talks, terrorist struck again in the valley. In a dozen separate attacks at least eighty people were killed .This was becoming a pattern – whenever bilateral discussions took place in New Delhi, the violence in Kashmir would escalate. When US Secretary of State Collin Powel came in October 2001, terrorists launched a grenade assault on the Jammu and Kashmir Assembly.

A few months later, the Parliament was attacked. Bombers entered the Indian parliament in a car and attempted to blow it up .They were killed by the police. Atal ji announced in the parliament that this time it will be *aar paar ki larai* and gave orders to the army to mobilize for a war. The waging of war has to be top confidential matter but it was blown out of proportion in the public and army was kept in high alert for 6 months but no war! What happens to the morale of our forces with this kind of approach! First giving the free passage to the enemy during Kargil after sacrificing 500 young – all below the age of 30 and then keep the army in high alert at the border for 6 months with no action. These wrong decisions which made the army and the people at large feel loss of pride was perhaps the most important reason for losing 2004 election under Atal ji. The country didn't approve of him for a second tenure and the BJP gave him Bharat Ratna after it came to power in 2014!.

Manmohan – mauni and mundane

Dr Manmohan Singh became the Prime Minister after Mrs. Sonia Gandhi declined and instead nominated him. He is a gentle soul, a brilliant economist, least greedy and has no hunger for power – great virtues. The economy was picking up globally after a bad recession of 98-03. Things were moving in the right direction. He continued to engage with Pakistan and was seen as a credible person. The Economy was opened up further and loan waivers of farmers to the tune of 73,000 crores were done. While the treasury had the money but the scheme was implemented in a hurry and loan was waived even for people who were in a position to pay.

This enabled the congress to win the election in 09. The other reasons for the win were getting the waiver for nuclear power project from US and a reputation he enjoyed among the global leaders as an intellectual and economist. In fact the second inning of congress was primarily because of him. Just before election, I was visited by a wandering Panditji from Balaji in AP and I asked him who is winning in the south. His response was an emphatic Dr Singh and when asked the reason, he said he has reached Delhi after travelling to major cities of Andhra

Pradesh, Karnataka and Maharashtra. People feel that it is for the first time that we have a Prime Minister who is respected globally and a gentleman – hence the vote is for Dr Singh.

Dr Singh again became the PM in 2009. One hoped that he will now assert himself as he did for getting the nuclear resolution. He had also gone for a heart surgery and one thought that with a stronger heart, he will be stronger too. But alas that didn't happen. Some good decisions including formation of NIA, designing GST and launching NAREGA were taken. GST was blocked by opposition but the other two were implemented. Shortcomings of NAREGA implementation were identified and audit started. J&K was under reasonable control and Naxals were identified as the biggest threat for the country.

However, BJP decided to create an atmosphere that the Govt was corrupt and they used CAG to inflict big time corruption charges on the Govt. 2G and Coalgate were on the top of the list. When coal gate losses were assessed around 270,00,000 crores, it was pointed out by some people that 50% of the blocks went to Coal India and that cannot be the part of the corruption, CAG immediately brought down the loss to 115,00,000 crores. There was no proof of money exchanging the hands.

The hypothesis of corruption was that if the resources were auctioned, they would have generated much higher value than the proceeds by allocating the resources. The assumption was that the allocations were made both for spectrum and coalfields to known people and perhaps by taking bribes. The spectrum was awarded to those who came first with the money and the rates were fixed. The coal mines leases were given to those who were recommended by the respective state Govts and mostly to the power projects. This was the basis being followed in the past. The opposition created a big ruckus and Supreme Court was approached which directed a JPC probe and CBI was asked to probe and cases were filed against Mr. Raja, then communication minster from the DMK. The spectrum and coal leases were cancelled. The spectrum was auctioned again and yielded less revenue and a payment phased out over a period of 10 years. Mr. Raja was exonerated by the CBI court and in coal gate, only couples of cases were filed. As far as the auction of coal block goes, there were no takers and coal import remains a big forex burden on the country. And there is no evidence that the money exchanged hands in either of the cases.

So the noise created on presumptuous CAG reports branding the Govt as the most corrupt and this was the single major factor for BJP coming to the power. CAG was duly rewarded by BJP with a Padm Bhushan and a role in BCCI. Congress couldn't propagate its good deeds and call the bluff of CAG. Dr Singh inability to speak and call the bluff resulted in Congress defeat.

Since Dr Singh remained silent and didn't assert himself, it was free for all in his cabinet. Cases of corruption, overlooking policies and favouratism were reported regularly. The moral of the story is that the "words" are important particularly when it comes to addressing large groups, a state or a nation i.e. in a leadership role. Action speaks louder than words is true in smaller groups – when the action can be seen and experienced directly. A leader definitely needs the words power in addition to good virtues and deeds. And since the leader kept *maun*, the other stalwarts of the party too remained *maun* instead of defending their Govt. "Yadadh Aachrate Shrestha....."

Modi – born Pracharak!

In his tenure as PM, Mr. Modi brought some good work ethics in the Govt including the discipline of timing and use of technology.

Ujawala, Crop, Life and health insurance were other good initiatives. The devil of course lies in implementation. Crop insurance is not working well. The quality and availability of doctors is a major constraint on the health front. Quality hospitals, private and public, are mainly in the big cities and metro. Unless the medical infrastructure is strengthened, including quality of doctors, the scheme may fall flat on its face. GST implementation was handled very casually and still suffers from some glitches. Welfare of poor is a good initiative and a vote catcher. All Govts including those in states have used this for remaining in power.

Modi ji with his experience and grounding as a *prcharak* was able to cast a magic spell and every one hoped that India now has a leader which will take the country to new heights and glory. He used social media extensively to propagate his views and thoughts. He came to power by blaming the Congress for all the ills of the country and projecting himself as an out of the world persona with 56 inch chest, a track record of developing Gujarat to a glorious state and a dream of serving the country. Disillusioned with Congress because of CAG reports and attracted by Modi ji's charisma, the public at large voted for BJP and the party came to power with a thumping majority.

However as a *Pracharak* is focused on speaking all the time and ensuring that the masses are galvanized, there is always a risk of committing more than what is feasible and even losing control over the tongue. Also to continue galvanizing the people, you use theatrics, develop new themes and make new promises all the time. Mr. Modi too used these tools extensively. In the beginning, he had new slogan every quarter – made in India, New India, Innovate India, Young India, Skill India, Stand up India and so on. By the middle of 2017 people realized that there were lot of *jumlas* and *jingoism* in his talks. Even in the rural India if you tried to fool a friend, the remark was, "do you think you are Modi"?

Thus truth – an important virtue for building a national character went for a toss.

A classic example is his announcement on 8th Nov 16. He started by saying that black money is normally stored in currency of bigger denominations and hence he has taken a call to demonetize the 1000 and 500 rupees notes. Then in the next sentence he said that he is introducing a 2000 rupees note! Wouldn't this help to create more black money? Poor and old people died in the lines for exchanging currency and he was heard saying that poor are having a sound sleep and riches are sleepless! Perhaps he was right - poor died and committed suicides – RIP, and the riches were busy planning which bank to bank upon, overseas or local branches. There have been deaths at regular intervals of suspected cattle smugglers. He said that the so called Gau Rakshaks were criminals but his ministers were hailing them all the time.

Arrogance was another vice displayed under his leadership. The PM himself says – *dekh lenge, mera bhi naam Modi hai* – not once but repeatedly. Mr. Jaitly commented on Supreme Court judges – *tyranny of unelected people*! A person reaches the level of Supreme Court judge after a long process of testing & selection. He forgot that he was a rejected and defeated candidate, and a minster through the Rajya Sabha route. Then we heard Mr. Gadkari saying that Navy needs to vacate the land in Mumbai and they are not required in Mumbai – instead they should be patrolling the coastal line of Pakistan. *Hamari sarkar hai aur hum land leke rahenge*! He was also heard telling a gathering of auto industry, both MNCs and Indians, that *mein tumhara band baza bajane wala hun*. Then there have been junior ministers, MPs, MLAs and the party workers speaking with the same arrogance. No one was spared – even the Nobel laureates like Amartya Sen and Mother Teresa.

Institutions were another casualty. A democracy lives through its institutions and building them by bringing the best leadership on the top, empowering them and strengthening them by appropriate policies & structure is required. We first saw premier institutions like IIMs and IITs getting interfered resulting in losing top notch professionals as Directors. This was followed by the universities. The long unrest in film institute in Pune because the Govt wanted a non entity as Director whereas the institute had a great lineage of distinguished directors.

The current state of CBI, CVC, RBI, CEC, ED, etc bears the Testimony to interfering and damaging the institutions. CBI had been branded as a caged Parrot by the Supreme Court during UPA time and now it was used as a coercion tool along with ED. Dinakaran, nephew of Shasikala and leader of breakaway AIDMK, was arrested and put behind bars for allegedly offering Rs 10,000 crores to Election Commission for getting the election symbol. After 2 days, he was released and no news on the case thereafter. It seems that this was a coercion tactic to get support of his MLAs for the President election. Mukul Roy and others from TMC were arrested under Sharada case and freed after they joined BJP.

Even Supreme Court was not spared – everyone remembers the four senior most judges addressing a press conference to inform the country that the democracy is under threat. A blunder which the country regrets even today was getting rid of Raghuram Rajan as Governor of RBI. We had an upright and competent Governor after a long time and we felt proud when the world complimented India for having the most competent governor of the central bank. The resignation of Mr. Urjit Patel was also for the reasons of interference.

So while the speed and bias for action was a welcome move, the country saw lies, arrogance, coercion and threats getting propagated! One hopes this doesn't become the norm for the future Govts. Again "Yaddhath Aachrati Shrestha, tattad evetaro janah. sa yat parmaana kurute, lokas tad anuvartate"

Bharat today – Raj mein Gunde, Dharam mein Pande and Samaj mein Andhe

———◆◆———

L et us look at the **Raj (Government)** first.

Legislature: The current legislators both in center and states comprise 35-40% people with civil & criminal cases against them. Some of them are being tried for murders, kidnapping & rapes. 25-30% are least interested in what is happening in the parliament/assemblies but the money and only a small percentage is serious about their role and participation.

Elected leaders are the real time leaders and their followers imitate their behavior and advocate their philosophy. MPs get their attendance marked even when they don't attend the parliament so that they get their allowances. You can call it a lie or a theft. The elected leaders thus are a symbol of lies, intolerance and violence. We have therefore developed a society which has very low tolerance and high arrogance. Rapes, murders, violence and other ills have grown. "Yaddhath Aachrati Shrestha, tattad evetaro janah. sa yat parmaana kurute, lokas tad anuvartate"

Why have we landed in this mess? Till the end of the late 50s, we were on the top of the global list on honesty and compassion. In a country so vast, have we run out of people who are honest and want to serve the country as its leaders and legislators! This needs a serious introspection and correction.

Executive: Executive has totally become subordinate to the legislator. We have seen good civil servants and police officers getting killed – either the culprits are not caught or the wheel of justice just doesn't move. Leaders with vested interests and their supporters have been abusing and beating officers resisting their wrong doings. Between 1995-2005, three chiefs in the health deptt in UP were murdered– one after another and no news of the culprits. So majority of the executive has aligned with the political bosses and the small minority of good officers is scared.

Mr P J Thomas, ex CVC, criticized the system for questioning him as head of country's top watchdog on corruption case since a large number of MPs also had cases against them. A person being tried in corruption cases becoming vigilance chief and defending himself ! Attorney General of UPA Govt told the S C bench in Sept 11 that there were 153 MPs at that point of time facing criminal cases, 74 of them for serious crimes like murder. He insisted that impeccable credentials were not a prerequiste and many judges would fail the test if similar yardstick was used to measure them. In 2010, tainted IAS officer AK Singh who was in Patna Jail for 2 months was appointed Jharkhand's Chief Secretary.

Army which is still fighting to maintain its reputation is also getting badly affected. In the current govt, we saw two retired Generals fighting elections – one won and became a minister and the other was defeated. After reaching to such a glory, why come to politics! Aren't you compromising your own prestige and that of the services? After being Chief of the Army, how does it sound being addressed as Neta ji! Does it speak well of a political party to give tickets to Generals and may be next time to a judge!

Judiciary: Mr. Shanti Bhushan, ex Law Minister and a practicing advocate for a long time gave an affidavit some years back confirming that out of the 32 CJIs till then, 16 were definitely corrupt, only 2 were clean and rest were under the suspicious category! The obvious question is why he didn't raise this during his tenure as Law Minister! However, this is true that judiciary too is inflicted with corruption and greed – more at junior level and less at senior level. The juniors would oblige the politicians, get promoted & become senior and will get used further. When you have people as judges whose integrity is doubtful, the casualty is the justice.

Justice is done when the punishment is given to the guilty. The murder is the most heinous crime and our jails are the safest club houses for the murderers. Jails allow you to eat what you want – home cooked food or even have a cook in the Jail (Shasikala's, ex AIDMK General Secretary, case an example), TV, Mobile, wife or girl friend visiting once in a while and anything on order if you can pay. They come out on parole, commit more crimes and go back to the safe heavens i.e **Jails.**

Each time you hear of a shootout in National Capital Region, the news is that the culprit has more than 2 dozen cases of murder and attempt to murder and was out on the parole. During the British Empire, one heard from the elders, that if a murder was not solved within a month, the commissioner of the area – a British - would jump into the fray and will not rest till the time it is solved. Unless immediate punishment is meted out to the murderers, how do we take care of law and order? The need is to sharpen the axe of punishment – justice means giving punishment to the guilty. It has to be immediate - otherwise it loses all its impact and relevance. Evidence & witnesses are manipulated or eliminated and there is no punishment.

The other issue is justice per say - everyone should be looked at with the same glasses! A few years back we had two most talked about cases in Noida in NCR – one involving Drs Talwars' daughter Arushi's murder and other about 54 odd kids getting killed in their neighborhood. Talwars case was pursued with vigor by everyone including media; the other case was left to die its own death. The main culprit here is Koli - non glamorous and with no godfather. He has already been awarded 4 death sentences and is being tried for more. Each time he gets a death sentence, he says I am innocent but who is interested in his story.

Another case which an upright judiciary would have taken up suo-moto, is that of Telagi. A real case of *Desh Droh*. Treasury and defence are two major responsibilities of a Govt. In this case our friend was printing stamp papers and some currency and selling this through a network and right inside the courts. He got the machines and toolings from a Government's printing press which as per the SOPs were to be destroyed! How did he manage to get these stamp papers sold inside the courts and why was the case left to die its own death. Telagi was enjoying a great life inside the jail till the time it got public that he is in the same jail as Shasikala and while Shasikala gets her cook, he gets his massage man every day inside the jail. Mr. Telagi was declared dead after a few days!

Telagi's case was something which showed the nexus of a large number of officials, politicians and people in judiciary. The media gave it some coverage in the beginning but blanked it out after one or two days. The case after the initial slow peddling went in the cold storage. I was feeling very restless at this and was keen to file a PIL in the Supreme Court. I talked to a few friends and their response was luke warm. After sometime, I happened to speak to someone who was shifting from Gurugram to Bangalore. I told him that it is good news as he will be closer to Chennai – his native place. He told me that he was at home in NCR too as his only sister lives here with her family. He also told me that his brother-in- law was a criminal lawyer in the Supreme Court. I told him about my agony on zero progress on Telagi's case and if he could check with his brother –in –law for filing a PIL.

He understood where I was coming from and promised that he will call me back in the next few days. I didn't hear from him for more than a fortnight and called him. I asked him if he thought I was drunk and being philosophical when I spoke to him. He said, no-no, - I could relate to your feelings and did speak with my brother-in-law but the reply he gave was disturbing – hence I didn't share with you. I requested him to tell me the reply he got and he said that his brother-in-law told him that it is an open secret in SC that no one will take or talk about Telagi's case.

Another interesting case is that of late Mr. Hiren Pandya. 8 people who were put in jail for his murder, were released by Gujarat high court as innocent. A promising young leader murdered and no clues on the culprits as yet. Another interesting case is that of Tehelaka editor – he has been in jail for years now on the charges of attempt to rape! Murderers walk freely and people for attempt to rape charge remain in Jail! On 1st May 2010, 3 high court PF scam tainted judges were reinstated by a collegium of 5 senior most judges a fortnight before the retirement of CJI Balakrishnan. Speaking on PF scam, the CJI had said in Dec 08, "every step will be taken to rid the judiciay of corrupt elements".

Now coming to Dharm: The dharm is not Hindu, Muslim or Christianity. It is a way of life for the human being as preached by great souls who incarnated for rejuvenating it from time to time. Unlike other creatures, who come loaded with fixed software of dharm, human beings have the freedom to choose their action. For example animals have their mating seasons whereas human beings can do it 24X7. A dog by and large would do *chowkidari* whereas a cat would be a *chor*.

The dharm got different names, by and large on the names of these incarnated souls. They appointed their torch bearers for carrying the path ahead. The torch bearers like Maulavis, Priests, Gurus, Sanyasis, Munis etc were to guide the human beings to move on the right path. However in today's scenario, majority of the torch bearers have degraded themselves. Some of them are in jails for variety of crimes – related to sex, murder and frauds. Still worse, when it comes to preaching, they teach *vairagya* to the *grihast* and *grihast* to their clan. The teachings are tailored for the audience and the place.

In a TV show, a Mahamandleswar and Maulana were participating. The anchor asked them about their opinion on freedom of friendship between the boys & girls – the Mandleswar said that he doesn't object to it if the intentions are good. The relationship between a young girl and a boy is that of fire and ghee. So what will the intentions do! Maulana said, we don't allow and the anchor said that you are taking us 5000 years back! A very celebrated and revered Guru recently said in a college that he doesn't believe in the cast system but the Lord says, "*chaturya varnam maya srista*". So all the torch bearers are saying what suits the audience so that they are not offended and remain their followers.

Sanyasis and Brahmins are the torch bearer of *Sanatana*. *Sanyasis* instead of living in secluded places and guiding the seekers are becoming one of them and Brahmins adjusting to their *Yajmans* wishes rather than guiding them correctly and firmly. And both have lost reputation. It is all about money!

And the Media: Media has the responsibility of bringing sanity in the society. Masses need insight on issues so that they don't become victims of mob mentality. The fourth pillar – representing *samaj has become andha.* Reasons are many - first again greed – will do anything for money. We have paid news, coerced news, fox syndrome news but no candid news. So the media is not helping the society in inculcating the right values but offering catchy news & stories to get their attention and improve – TRP, Circulation,

Glamour, etc. Debates are de passé, noisy fights are on, sanity has gone to dogs, vanity is the flavor and we have a set of youngsters managing the show – the wisdom of experience and grey hairs is story of "once upon a time". It is the lungs power rather than experience and wisdom.

This all has happened in the 21st century. In late 90s, I was in London and saw a leading daily carrying a story about Lady Diana having a mole on her thigh! I joked with my friend about standard of media in Great Britain and told him that forget about the front page, this kind of news will not find any place in our media. Today, we have passed all the limits of being civil and the media is competing with each other to carry more of glamour and nudity. Some of our leading news papers are Tabloids! No serious content business – recycle and recycle again. The onslaught of internet has added a new level to the vulgarity in our society. TV news has become a Tamasha Video except for a few exceptions. Fox syndrome is experienced every day.

So the Media which once guided the masses at large today doesn't know what should be given the coverage, how to deliberate and is at the brink of losing its credibility. The watch-dog of the society has become *Andha*.

The Path Ahead

Rejuvenating Bharat

How do we reach to our past glory – an India which Lord Macaulay saw in 1832 - less than 200 years ago? Forget about 1832, till 1950 India was full of compassion, truth and lived in a pious manner. The decay stared in 70s, got accelerated in 90s and is hitting the roof top in 21st century. We still have some hope left provided we make correct move to rejuvenate it.

Is it the leadership or the society which will bring this change? You talk about corruption or lack of character in any institution, the standard reply from people at the helm of affairs is that this is the kind of people society is producing today. Leaders blame society and society towards the leadership. So it is the chicken vs egg story. Both have important role - character building will start from the society and leaders will have to lead by example.

Issue of Leadership

The leadership issue at the national level is the PM and the MPs. We need these leaders with wisdom, values and compassion. In a vast country like ours, are we sort of people who want to give some years of their lives for serving the country? Definitely not! However the reality is that 35-40% of the MPs today have criminal records. The balance 35-40% are fence sitters and only 15- 20% have good character and intentions. This miniscule group cannot do much as their voice is curtailed by the majority.

The entry of tainted leaders started in 70s, went to 15% in the 80s and grew at a fast pace during and after 90s. The criminals in the legislature grew after the development fund for each MP and MLA was started by Mr. Narsimha Rao in 90s. The value of fund has gone up substantially since then and it makes sense for criminals to make easy money instead of indulging in robbery and abduction. The fund is a big waste as 20 -50% of this is kept for distribution amongst various stake holders at the time of disbursal. The balance money is partly deployed on projects and the remaining distributed amongst the village level leaders including Gram Pradhan and the people who championed getting the project from MP or MLA. Former CJI, Justice ES Venkataramiah called this scheme "assaulting the constitution". It enables MPs and MLAs to woo voters, look after their supporters and facilitates corruption. It also makes mockery of the panchayati raj. Abolishing this fund would be a good step to clean the legislatures and spare money for productive investment – generating revenue and employment.

The other action required is stricter norms on eligibility – to start with disqualifying anyone with a criminal case in the court. The media and the society need to create awareness about tainted people getting fielded by each party – putting both the parties and individuals to name and shame. This will affect the individuals as well as the parties' share of votes for sure. Majority of the country even today supports good values and good people. This will force parties to select or even invite good people to join the rank. .

The PM is a bigger issue. As we saw in our analysis of leaders till today, each one of them influenced the society positively or negatively by their deeds and words. PM is the real leader of the nation at a given point of time and as the Lord had said, the society follows the leader, "Yadadh Aachrate Shrestha.....". If we could get PMs of character and values, we would be half-way on the path to rejuvenation. In the current system, we even have had compromised candidates as PM in the past and the history may repeat itself!

We need to seriously review the current system and explore the possibility of a Presidential system. This will ensure that we get a person elected by direct voting and this country will pick a person of character and values. We can have a system wherein a person needs more than 50% votes to get elected. In case of a fractured voting; the top two contestants can go for a revote as is the practice in some European nations and even in Afghanistan. The advantages are many:

- The person will definitely be seen and accepted as a national leader and will have influence across the country. This is particularly important to keep the country united as most of the States are going to be controlled by regional parties with their own agenda.
- The President will have a term of full 5 years irrespective of parties' positions in the Parliament
- The President can pick his team of specialists and hence deliver better.
- We will have a real leader and not a compromised candidate at the helm of the affairs.
- The executive will be out of politicians clutches and empowered.

There have been noises on this even earlier. A private member bill was moved for a Presidential system in the parliament in the past. Mr. Ram Jethmalani made 3 suggestions in Rajya Sabha in August 11 and one of them was direct election of PM. What is the way out! Parliament constituting a constitution review committee to examine the Presidential system. The Constitution needs a review even otherwise as it has been amended many times. We also need to see how key institutions can be empowered. If Parliament doesn't do it, an appeal can be made to the President by collecting signatures of large chunk of voters from across the country, to ask EC to conduct a referendum.

Towards a civic society

Society's structure has changed – we no more live in joint families where the elders and children were together and they got the wisdom of experiential learning from the elders. Right values were inculcated and nourished. Family is the 1st unit/institution and this is where the foundation of a good society is laid. The learning from the family has been further vitiated by media and internet. Parents and kids both are busy with their gadgets – scanning through good, bad and the ugly. If the joint family system was functioning, we would perhaps have not reached this stage.

Today the only way to rejuvenate the society is education - bringing life to a currently dead system. There is no direction, no objective for each stage of education and no differentiation between Vidhya *and Education* (Knowledge). Media has been reporting regularly that 7th standard kids can't read 2nd standard texts and can't do simple math. So forget Vidhya, even knowledge is not there!

We need to reboot the system totally. Focus on developing interest in learning, ability to read & write and do numericals at the primary stage, laying foundation for developing citizens who will do good to the self and to the society during the middle stage and to develop *patarta* (career skills) in the senior school. *Vidya dadati vinayam, vinayat jaati patartam, patarta dhanam aapunoti, dhanaat dharmam tathh sukham.* The education till middle should be the focus of the Govt. Standard syllabus, selection process of teachers so that we really get real gurus as teachers and a good leadership at the supervisory level **will make it possible.**

For middle education to deliver a civic society, the focus should be on acquiring a holistic knowledge of the body, mind and soul. We should bring all the teachings of different Religions and impart this knowledge. This is the right age to learn and develop values & character. All the religions teach Non- violence, truth and compassion.

"Ahinsa parmo dharm, ahinsa parmo damh, Ahinsa parmam daan, ahinsa parmam taph:"

"satyam brahm, taph satya, satyam visrijate praja, satyam dharyate loka, swarg satyam gachjhati".

(Mahabharat)

All religion teach respect to elders e,g. Manusmriti says, "Abhivaadan-sheelasy, nityo-bridhop-sevinh, chatwari tasya vridhyante, aayur-vidhya-yasho-balam".

The four key tasks of human being – arth, kaam, dharm and moksha all are dependent on a healthy body and this must get adequate focus in the middle school. Appreciation of *niyamas* and *yamas* – described under different names in various religions should also be part of the syllabus. All religions talk about heaven and hell, and moksha. It is only the human race which can and must try for heaven if not moksha. Otherwise life is a waste:

"Maanushy yah samaasaadhy swarg-moksh prasaadhakam, dwayor na saadhyedek, ten atmaa vanchit dhruvam".

Garur Puran

To reach a perfect level of body, mind and soul, our 7 energy chakras must be energized. This can only be done if we pronounce all the 52 *akshar* - not restrict to 26 alphabets of English. This brings us to refocusing on Sanskrit. Today some universities in Europe are doing a much better job on teaching & research in Sanskrit than in India. It is interesting that even Mr. Subhash Chandra Bose studied Sanskrit in Paris during his stay there.

Matur is a village in Shimoga district in Karnataka state, known for the usage of Sanskrit for day-to-day communication, although the general language of the state is Kannada. Mostly toppers of secondary school and universities of the state are from this village. They are employed in the best of the companies globally. People in the village feel that this is primarily because of Sanskrit. Mastery over grammar of Sanskrit as defined by Panigrihi will enlighten a person to become totally tuned to the science of Parkriti – nature, the *Vidhya*. Sanskrit has the potential of becoming a programming language which can be a great advantage to India. Even if we develop 25 - 30% of our next generation as reasonably enlightened, it would be good enough to spread the light across the society.

In other words, middle education – the right age to inculcate values & virtues, should bring the best teachings of all the religions on body, mind & soul and create a healthy and civic society. It will also create an atmosphere of *sarv dharm sambhaav* and since everyone will have the same education, hopefully the current reservation system may go from the country as everyone will have the same education.

Conclusion

"So we have really landed in a big soup. Legislative, Executive, Judiciary and Media, all are in a decay. Air, water, Food, education, governance, law & order and everything else is heavily polluted and corrupted. No one talks about these burning issues because we have Raj Mein Gunde, Dharm mein Pande, Samaj mein Andhe - a true description of our current state." The cultured society which Macaulay talked had Indians who lived according to the human dharma. Bharat was the spiritual leader and guide to the humanity at large. We need to go back to the basics if we want our Bharat to again become a place which is revered by one and all because of its knowledge, culture – way of life and above all for its humane values.

The prerequisites are a capable leadership and a civic society. We are not short of good leaders – we see examples everywhere in academics, social service, sports, industry and Govt. A presidential system will bring good people to the fore for leadership at national level. A big noise level on corrupt candidates by media and amendments in the EC rules will ensure parties field cleaner candidates for parliament.

Civic society will be developed by an objective driven middle school education. Assuming that we need five years time to develop all the apparatus for this and then run this for the 1st batch of middle school, the students will be ready to influence the society by the time they reach 17-18. We will start seeing the results in 10 – 12 years time – not a long period.

"We the people" have a responsibility to nurture the democracy which we got after a long struggle - long revolution and then evolution. We don't need any revolution or evolution now but a rejuvenation attempt. Each one of us has a morale responsibility to protect what we got – democracy, the best suited Govt system for civic and enlightened society. A gift from the Almighty and our forefathers! During the freedom struggle each one participated, academics, bureaucrats, lawyers, industrialists – Birlas and Bajaj were key supporters of Gandhi ji, peasants, leaders from all walks of life and from across the regions and religions.

The task today is easy - galvanizing self and others in our circles to rejuvenate Bharat to achieve the following objectives:

- A Presidential system.
- Members of Parliament – people of values and in a position to give 5 -10 years of their lives in the service of the motherland. 545 civic and cultured people will do great good to the country instead of getting party based candidates. National Govts in some of the European countries have done much better and imagine a national government comprising of honest- enlightened people with burning desire to serve the country.
- Rebooting the education system to create a healthy and compassionate society – each member able to pursue the four objectives of human life - *arth, dharm, kam* and *moksha.* Thus creating a society in which "*sarvey bhavantu sukhino, sarvey bhavantu niramaya, sarvey bhavantu bhadrani, maa kaschit dukh bha bhavet*" will become a reality.

Democracy is a gift of the Almighty to us for which many angels incarnated in this land including universal adult franchise which didn't happen even in US . Taking money for votes and voting for criminals, will definitely lead to punishment here and beyond. If we observe closely, we can see this happening already to people who are not following the duty of protecting the gift of the Almighty.

We are responsible for where we are today either by committing the crime of destroying the democracy or by being indifferent to what is happening. It is our pious duty to take corrective action and if we don't, we will carry the guilt till the end of this life and beyond.

If we don't make a move now, it may be too late. Let us start now with a small step to commit to the rejuvenation movement by sending a mail, "I commit to rejuvenating of my country" at rejuvenatingbharat@gmail.com. And ask friends and fraternity to do the same. Please do it now irrespective of your age, stature, location and profession. "We the people" includes all.

Once we reach a threshold level of affirmations, the next course of action will emerge. Almighty will bless us in achieving the goal.

www.ingramcontent.com/pod-product-compliance
Lightning Source LLC
Chambersburg PA
CBHW060235180626
46813CB00007B/3098